For Joy Backhouse

First published in Great Britain in 1990
by Methuen Children's Books Ltd
Michelin House, 81 Fulham Road, London SW3 6RB
Illustrations copyright © 1990 by Francesca Crespi
Text copyright © 1990 by Jean Richardson
Printed and bound in Hong Kong

ISBN 0 416 15822 6

The Nutcracker

THE STORY OF TCHAIKOVSKY'S BALLET

Retold by Jean Richardson

Illustrated by

Francesca Crespi

Methuen Children's Books

It was the most magical day of the year –
Christmas Eve – and cold enough for snow.

But neither Clara nor her brother Fritz had
time to watch the snowflakes, because they
were getting ready for a party.

Clara couldn't make up her mind which
ribbon to wear with her new frock. Fritz, who
was dressed as a soldier, kept teasing her by
brandishing his sword.

Their parents had invited all their friends and relations to the party.

There were dozens of cousins, aunts old and young, uncles fat and thin, two short plump grandmas and a whiskery grandpa.

Clara looked at the presents under the Christmas tree for the umpteenth time. She particularly wanted to be sure there was a present for the mysterious Herr Drosselmeyer, one of her father's oldest friends and Clara's favourite guest.

There were mountains of food: pastry that concealed the tenderest meat; puddings studded with raisins and nuts of every sort; trifles and jellies; mince tarts and candied fruits.

And when the guests weren't eating or drinking, or gossiping or flirting, or opening their presents, they whirled their way through the latest waltzes and polkas.

But where was Herr Drosselmeyer? Clara was afraid that perhaps he wasn't coming.

Then suddenly he appeared in the doorway – looking more mysterious than ever.

He always brought Clara a surprise, and she was longing to know what it was.

Herr Drosselmeyer was amused by her impatience. He put his hand in his pocket and brought out...

…a firework that burst into pink and green stars! Clara was enchanted.

All the children gathered round him as handkerchiefs disappeared into thin air and coloured balls vanished behind his ears or slipped into his elbows.

Finally, from pockets as deep as sacks, came the presents.

There were toy soldiers for Fritz,
clockwork toys for the cousins, and for
Clara, something very special.

The box gave no clue to what it
contained, and everyone was curious as
Clara lifted the lid.

Inside was the strangest doll she had
ever seen. It was a small pair of
nutcrackers decorated with the face
and uniform of a handsome soldier.
Clara fell in love with him at once.

"He's the captain of my soldiers," Fritz shouted, snatching the doll from Clara and darting round the room.

When she finally caught him, Clara twisted his arm

until he let go of the doll, which fell on the floor. When she picked the Nutcracker up, one of his arms had broken.

Clara burst into tears.

"Let me see," said Herr Drosselmeyer, taking the doll gently from Clara. "Soldiers must expect to be wounded, but I think, with a little magic, we can make him better."

He took out a little jar smelling of herbs, rubbed some cream on the arm and tied it in position with Clara's handkerchief. "There, put him somewhere safe, and he'll be as good as new by tomorrow morning."

Clara laid the Nutcracker tenderly back in his box and put it on a high shelf. Her father warned Fritz not to touch it.

Clara was so worried about the Nutcracker that she couldn't sleep. She felt she must steal downstairs and make sure he was all right.

The sleeping house looked ghostly and unfamiliar. The drawing-room was peopled with shadows and moonlight silvered the Christmas tree.

As Clara reached up for the Nutcracker's box, the grandfather clock struck midnight and the strangest things began to happen.

First, the Christmas tree began to grow, until
Clara could only just see the star on the top.
And it went on unfolding, higher and higher…
Next, she heard scuffles, and a troop of mice as
tall as she was tumbled down the chimney.
They scurried to the table and began helping
themselves to food, giggling with greedy
delight.

Suddenly one of them saw Clara and pointed
her out to his friends. The moonlight glinted on
claws and teeth as they moved towards her.

Clara screamed.

Instantly Fritz's regiment of toy soldiers sprang
to her rescue. They surrounded Clara and
began to attack the mice with their swords. The
mice fought back with their teeth and claws
and used their tails to trip up the soldiers.
    The mice seemed to be winning.

But Clara had forgotten about the Nutcracker. Suddenly he sprang out of his box and took command.

He ordered his soldiers to make ready the cannon, and then led them into battle. Now his men were as fearless and agile as he, and soon most of the mice had been bowled over or taken prisoner.

Only the Mouse King remained, and he challenged the Nutcracker to a duel.

Although the Nutcracker still had his arm in a sling, he fought bravely. His sword scissored through the air, narrowly missing the Mouse King's whiskers.

The Mouse King's tail snaked across the floor. Clara

saw the Nutcracker catch his feet in it. As he fell and
the Mouse King pounced, she threw her shoe, hitting
the Mouse King on the head. At that moment the
cannon exploded in a puff of smoke.

When the smoke cleared, the mice and the soldiers had disappeared, and the Nutcracker, taller and even more handsome, was dressed as a prince.

"You saved my life," he said, and bowed low.

"Now, to thank you, I would like to take you on a journey to the Kingdom of Sweets."

Clara saw that a sleigh was waiting for them. As it flew through the air, she was covered by a cloak of snowflakes as warm as feathers.

They were welcomed by the Sugar Plum Fairy,
who had arranged an entertainment for them.
    While Clara and the Prince sat side by side
on golden thrones, all Clara's favourite sweets
danced for them.

Finally, the Prince asked Clara to dance. Her feet seemed bewitched as she twirled on her points and then floated through the air as light as swansdown. The Prince's eyes told her that she looked beautiful, and they might have been dancing together all their lives.

When Clara awoke on Christmas morning, she
was back in bed and Fritz had started opening
his presents.

Could it have been just a dream, she
wondered? But there was something under her
pillow.

It was the Nutcracker doll, and she saw at
once that his arm had mended and he was as
good as new.